CHESTER'S WAY

by Kevin Henkes

Puffin Books

PUFFIN BOOKS

A Division of Penguin Books USA Inc.
375 Hudson Street, New York, New York 10014
Penguin Books Ltd, 27 Wrights Lane, London W8 5TZ, England
Penguin Books Australia Ltd, Ringwood, Victoria, Australia
Penguin Books Canada Ltd, 10 Alcorn Avenue, Toronto, Ontario, Canada M4V 3B2
Penguin Books (N.Z.) Ltd, 182–190 Wairau Road, Auckland 10, New Zealand

Penguin Books Ltd, Registered Offices: Harmondsworth, Middlesex, England

First published in the United States of America by Greenwillow Books,
a division of William Morrow & Company, Inc. 1988
Published by arrangement with William Morrow & Company, Inc.
Published in Picture Puffins 1989
10
Copyright © Kevin Henkes, 1988
All rights reserved

LIBRARY OF CONGRESSS CATALOGING-IN-PUBLICATION DATA
Henkes, Kevin.   Chester's way / Kevin Henkes.   p.   cm.
Summary: Chester and Wilson share the same exact way of doing
things, until Lilly moves into the neighborhood and shows them that
new ways can be just as good.
ISBN 0-14-054053-9
[1. Friendship—Fiction.   2. Mice—Fiction.]   I. Title.
[PZ7.H389Ch   1989]   [E]—dc20   89-32427

Printed in Hong Kong by South China Printing Co.
Set in ITC Galliard

• For Ginny •

Hello, my name is Chester.
I like croquet and peanut butter
and making my bed.

CHESTER had his own way of doing things....

He always cut his sandwiches
diagonally.

He always got out of bed
on the same side.

And he never left the house
without double-knotting his shoes.

Chester always had the same thing for breakfast—toast with jam and peanut butter.

And he always carried a miniature first-aid kit in his back pocket. Just in case.

"You definitely have a mind of your own," said Chester's mother. "That's one way to put it," said Chester's father.

Chester's best friend Wilson was
exactly the same way. That's why
they were best friends.

Chester wouldn't play baseball
unless Wilson played, and they
never swung at the first pitch
or slid headfirst.

Wilson wouldn't ride his bike
unless Chester wanted to, and
they always used hand signals.

If Chester was hungry, Wilson was too, but they rarely ate between meals.

"Some days I can't tell those two apart," said Wilson's mother. "Me either," said Wilson's father.

Chester and Wilson, Wilson and Chester. That's the way it was.

They loved to go on picnics. Once,
when Wilson accidently swallowed
a watermelon seed and cried
because he was afraid that a
watermelon plant would grow
inside him, Chester swallowed
one, too.
"Don't worry," said Chester.
"Now, if you grow a watermelon
plant, I'll grow one, too."

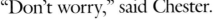

Chester duplicated his Christmas
list every year and gave a copy
to Wilson, because they always
wanted the same things anyway.

For Halloween, they always dressed as things that went
together—salt and pepper shakers, two mittens on a
string, ham and eggs.
"They really are two peas in a pod," said Chester's mother.
"Looks like it," said Chester's father.

In spring, Chester and Wilson shared the same umbrella.

In winter, they never threw snowballs at each other.

In fall, they raked leaves together.

And in summer, they reminded each other
to wear sunscreen, so they wouldn't burn.

Chester and Wilson, Wilson and Chester.
That's the way it was.

And then Lilly moved into the neighborhood.

LILLY had <u>her</u> own way of doing things....

She wore band-aids all over her
arms and legs, to look brave.

I MA YLLIL

She talked backwards to herself
sometimes, so no one would
know what she was saying.

And she never left the house
without one of her
nifty disguises.

Lilly waved at all the cars that passed by, even if she didn't know who was in them.

And she always carried a loaded squirt gun in her back pocket. Just in case.

"She definitely has a mind of her own," said Chester.
"That's one way to put it," said Wilson.

When Lilly asked Chester and Wilson to play, they
said they were busy.

When she called them up on the phone, they disguised
their voices and said they weren't home.

If Lilly was walking on one side of the street, Chester
and Wilson crossed to the other and hid.

"She's something else," said Chester.
"Looks like it," said Wilson.

One day, while Chester and Wilson were practicing their hand signals, some older boys rode by, popping wheelies. They circled Chester and Wilson and yelled personal remarks.

Chester and Wilson didn't know what to do. Just when
they were about to give up hope, a fierce-looking cat with
horrible fangs jumped out of the bushes and frightened
the older boys away.

"Are you who I think you are?" Chester asked the cat.
"Of course," the cat replied.

"Thank you, Lilly," said Chester.

"You're welcome, Chester," said Lilly.

"Thank you, Lilly," said Wilson.

"You're welcome, Wilson," said Lilly.

"I'm glad you were wearing a disguise," said Chester.

"And I'm glad you had your squirt gun," said Wilson.

"I always do," said Lilly. "Just in case."

Afterward, Chester invited
Lilly over for lunch.
"<u>You</u> have a Muscle Mouse
cup?!" said Lilly.
"Of course," said Chester.
"I do, too!" said Lilly.
"Same here," said Wilson.

Chester and Wilson cut their
sandwiches diagonally. Lilly asked
Chester's mother if she had cookie
cutters, and she made stars and
flowers and bells.
"That's neat!" said Chester.
"Wow!" said Wilson.

That night, Lilly invited Chester
and Wilson to sleep over.
"<u>You</u> have a night light?!" said
Chester.
"Of course," said Lilly.
"I do, too!" said Chester.
"Same here," said Wilson.

Chester and Wilson wanted toast
with jam and peanut butter for
breakfast the next morning.
"Boring," said Lilly. "Try this
instead."
"This is good!" said Chester.
"Wow!" said Wilson.

After that, when Lilly asked
Chester and Wilson to play,
they said yes.

When she called them up on
the phone, they had pleasant
conversations.

And if Lilly was walking on one
side of the street, Chester and
Wilson waved and ran to catch
up with her.

Chester and Wilson taught Lilly hand signals. And she taught them how to pop wheelies.

Lilly taught Chester and Wilson how to talk backwards. And they taught her how to double-knot her shoes.

"Some days I can't tell those three apart," said
  Lilly's mother.
"Me either," said Lilly's father.

Chester and Wilson and Lilly, Lilly and Wilson
and Chester. That's the way it was.

For Halloween, they dressed as The Three Blind Mice.

For Christmas, Lilly gave Chester and Wilson nifty disguises. And they gave her a box of multi-colored shoelaces—extra long for double-knotting.

They loved to go on picnics. When Chester and Wilson told Lilly about how they had each swallowed a watermelon seed once, Lilly swallowed <u>three</u> of them. "I'll grow a watermelon plant for each of us," she said.

In spring, Chester and Wilson and Lilly shared the same umbrella.

In winter, they never threw snowballs at each other.

In fall, they raked leaves together.

And in summer, they reminded each other to wear sunscreen, so they wouldn't burn.

Chester and Wilson and Lilly,
Lilly and Wilson and Chester.
That's the way it was. . . .

And then Victor moved into the neighborhood...